LindaRoach

The Busiest Boy in Holland

by LISL WEIL

1964 FIRST CADMUS EDITION
THIS SPECIAL EDITION IS PUBLISHED BY ARRANGEMENT WITH
THE PUBLISHERS OF THE REGULAR EDITION
HOUGHTON MIFFLIN COMPANY
BY
E. M. HALE AND COMPANY
EAU CLAIRE, WISCONSIN

THE BUSIEST BOY IN HOLLAND

Written and Illustrated by Lisl Weil

Toontje, a little Dutch boy, was always busy — busy imagining things like pushbutton ice skates that make him travel like the wind, or fishnets with magnets that attract eels out of the sea. The biggest day in Holland was the Flower Festival, when huge floats of flowers were paraded in Amsterdam before the crowds and the Royal Family. Toontje and his brothers helped their uncle on his tulip farm and made their own float for the Festival. As they were parading, their float started to leak, and Toontje saved the float in an old-fashioned way, like the little boy who saved Holland from the flood in the famous story, and became a new hero.

K

Dewey Decimal Classification: E

About the Author and Illustrator:

LISL WEIL was born in Vienna, Austria, and came to the United States in 1939. She was educated in Vienna, and while in school was drawing and illustrating for well-known magazines and newspapers. Her work has been exhibited widely on the Continent, and she has traveled widely. She found that drawing for children made her happiest, and has also written some of the books she has illustrated, as *The Busiest Boy In Holland*. During one year she had a story telling television show, and for ten years she was with the Thomas Scherman's Little Orchestra, drawing the story of the music for their Society Concerts for Young People. She lives in New York City.

On the island of Marken, across the Zuider Zee from Volendam, lives a little Dutch boy named Toontje. To him, there can be no better place in the whole world to live. His three brothers and two sisters, his mother and father think so too. So does his grandfather, who has lived on Marken all his life as his father had before him.

And so does Albert. Only Albert lives in a tub. He is Toontje's pet goldfish.

In all the houses all around them lived Toontje's first, second, and third cousins, his aunts and uncles — in short, everybody except Uncle Johannes who lives far away in Hillegom, beyond the big city of Amsterdam.

2

Everybody on Marken is related to everybody else, like a big happy family. They bustle about on weekdays and Sundays, always busy doing something.

But Toontje is really the busiest boy in all of Holland. Even when he seems to be doing nothing.

Then it is that Toontje keeps so still he doesn't even move a finger. He sits quietly looking away out over the dike and beyond the sea . . . busy imagining all sorts of things. The quieter Toontje becomes, the bigger and more impossible his ideas get.

4

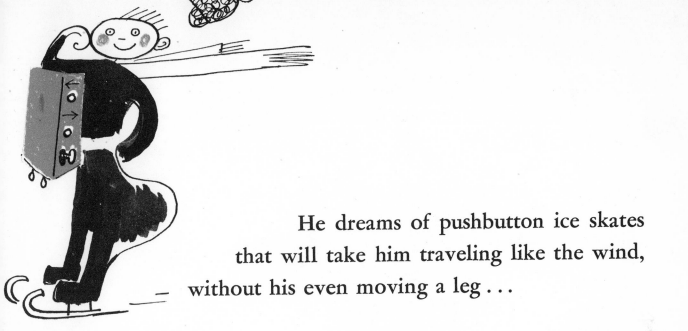

He dreams of pushbutton ice skates
that will take him traveling like the wind,
without his even moving a leg . . .

or fishnets with magnets
that will attract eels and herring
right out of the sea . . .

Sometimes Toontje's head is so full of new schemes that he almost forgets to bring Albert into the house in the evening. Once he did forget, and poor Albert would have been a dead fish if the rain had not come pelting down. And a good thing it did. For water, of course, is what Albert needs — while it keeps all the cats at a safe distance.

Rain isn't enough, though, to keep everything spick and span as it ought to be in Holland. The washing and scrubbing and polishing are never done.

One day when Toontje was helping his sisters with the scrubbing, they heard him muttering to himself: "Someday I will find an easier way — I'll figure out a big machine with five brushes and five mops to do all the cleaning by itself."

His sisters shook their heads: "That Toontje, he is always dreaming of new ways to do things — are the old ways not good enough for you, Toontje?"

Toontje never seemed to hear them,
nor did he hear his brother Kees calling, until
Kees had shouted three times.
"Come quickly," yelled Henk,
"We've got a letter from Uncle Johannes," Jan bellowed
at the top of his lungs.

It was a few minutes before Toontje could take in what
his brothers were trying to tell him: that Uncle Johannes
needed help with the tulip crop. It was almost time for
the Flower Festival and there was so much work to do.
Could he borrow Kees, Jan, Henk, and Toontje for two
weeks? In return, Uncle Johannes would help them to
make a float to take in the Parade.

Why, the only time they had
been away was to
Middelburg —
a little trip only.

How exciting to go on a big trip, way over to the big
city of Amsterdam! And to have their own float of flowers
to parade before the Queen!

Father just couldn't say no, could he?

He couldn't.

"Let's make a float of daffodils in the shape of a duck-
ling," said Kees.

"No, let's make a boat with sails of red tulips."

"I know, I know," said Jan, talking so fast and jumping
about so that everyone just had to listen. "We will be a
long way from home and we . . ." "Shush," interrupted
Toontje, "that's it — but let's keep it a secret."

10

The next few days
were busy ones
for all of them,
but not once did they give away their secret.

Soon it was time to leave. Practically all the family came
to see them off on the boat. The boys, dressed in their best
Sunday clothes, carried mysterious-looking bundles on
their bikes.

Toontje held his with great care.

"Goodbye, goodbye. We'll see you at the Parade,"

shouted all the first, second and third cousins, the aunts and
uncles and grandfather, too. For this year all the relatives
wanted to go to the big Flower Festival.

Did they not have to see their own boys in the Parade?
What's more, everyone was curious to see the secret float.

13

When the boat landed right in the big city of Amsterdam,

Toontje and his brothers still had not told their secret to anyone.

Never before had they seen so many people. It was not easy to pedal their way through the crowds.

Finally they were alongside the dike on the road to
Uncle Johannes' tulip farm.

How happy Uncle Johannes was to see them.

Right away they all set to work,

picking tulips, pulling up bulbs,

and loading the boats for market.

18

Now and then Toontje would get that faraway look but his brothers would poke him in the ribs: "No time for dreaming, Toontje. Only six days to go."

While all hands worked, people talked about the Parade and the floats: "There'll be an enormous fish, all made out of hyacinths, and it will move its tail!"

"There'll be a Giant Snowman, as big
as a house," said another.

"There'll be a ship right out of the
Arabian Nights," said a third.

Three days to go.

Every night after work, Uncle Johannes helped the boys with their float. What with painting of this and that, and making the floor strong enough to hold their surprise, there was enough work to keep everyone busy.

Finally, the big day was TOMORROW,

The Great Day AT LAST!

All through the village and, from all the surrounding villages, the Parade formed in long lines past miles and miles of flower beds. On the sidelines were crowds of people — all the world had come to watch the Parade, or so it seemed to the boys from the Island of Marken.

And close on the heels

of the Giant Snowman came

a miniature float of the Island of Marken.
Houses on stilts —
    painted doors and windows —

boats — nets — and water all around
with a real fish in it.
    Fish? Yes, Albert is the fish.

Everyone clapped hands and shouted, "Hooray for the boys of Marken!" Even louder shouted all the first, second, and third cousins; the aunts and uncles and grandfather. Mother and father and sisters too glowed with pride.

Then all of a sudden, all the people began to laugh.

What could they be laughing about?

The boys looked around at the crowd —
everyone was pointing . . .

— laughing and making fun of THEIR little Island of
Marken.

Oh, what a disgrace!

Toontje looked down at the float, and his heart skipped
a beat.

The water was slowly dripping out of the float,

drop

by

drop.

Albert would be a dead fish by the time they passed
before the royal family.

"Whatever are we going to do?" wailed Henk.

"We've got to save Albert!" cried Kees, getting off his bicycle and crawling under the float.

"I'll hold Albert in my hand," said Jan.

"No, no!" insisted Toontje, "if you take him out of the water he will surely die."

All the floats behind them had stopped. People were stretching their necks to see what the trouble was.

But Toontje did not notice. He jumped off his bike at once, found the hole where a knot in the wood had dropped out, and

PUT his finger in the hole.

"The water has stopped dripping," yelled Kees from under the float. He got up to see what had happened. Jan and Henk were staring, their mouths wide open. Toontje was getting onto his bike again, saying "Come on, let's go."

As the float passed before the reviewing stand, there was another burst of applause.

"Bravo, Toontje," shouted the crowds. Toontje held on . . . Only once he did look up, just long enough to see the royal family. Then he turned back to keep his eyes on Albert.

It was not easy
to ride his bike and stop the leak at the same time but Toontje held on, quietly and steadily, till

the float paraded right back to Uncle Johannes' farm.

"Well done, Toontje," Uncle Johannes called out. "You saved the day."

"And Albert too," laughed Toontje.

Then, tired and stiff as he was, he smiled at his sisters: "You see, there are times when the old ways are good enough for me."

At this everyone burst into laughter, for they knew Toontje was thinking of the famous story of the little Dutch boy who long ago had saved Haarlem from a terrible flood by stopping a leak in the dike with his finger.

And now the people of Marken would have a real story
to tell about their own hero — the busiest boy in Holland.

Albert, meanwhile,

    kept swimming about in

his own little Zuider Zee

    without a care in the world.

LIBRARY OF CONGRESS CATALOG CARD NUMBER: 59–5191

This edition lithographed in U. S. A. by Wetzel Bros., Inc., Milwaukee 2, Wisconsin

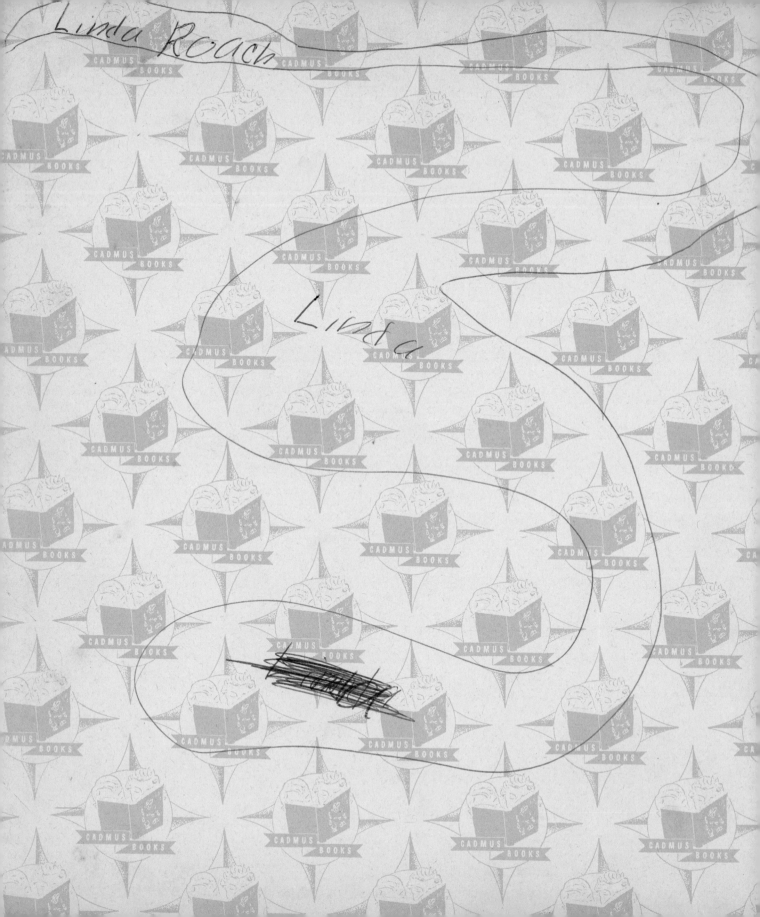